THE AUNTS GO MARCHING

Maurie J. Manning

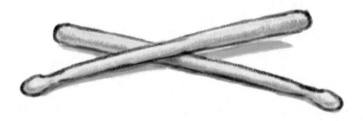

SCHOLASTIC INC.

New York   Toronto   London   Auckland   Sydney
Mexico City   New Delhi   Hong Kong   Buenos Aires

For Kathy, Kay, Eileen, Judy, and all my aunts.
And in loving memory of Aunt Mary.

—M. J. M.

ISBN 0-439-64007-5

12 11 10 9 8 7 6 5 4 3 2 1   4 5 6 7 8 9/0

Printed in the U.S.A.   40

First Scholastic printing, March 2004

The text of this book is set in 16-point Caxton Book.

Rat a tat-tat!

Rat a tat-tat!

Ba-rump, ba-rump,

b a - r u m p !

The aunts go marching one by one, hurrah! Hurrah!
The aunts go marching one by one, hurrah! Hurrah!
The aunts go marching one by one.
The little one stops to bang on her drum.
And they all go marching down to the town
in the rain, in the rain.

Rat a tat-tat! Rat a tat-tat! Ba-rump, ba-rump, ba-rump!

The aunts go marching two by two, hurrah! Hurrah!
The aunts go marching two by two, hurrah! Hurrah!
The aunts go marching two by two.
The little one stops to fix her shoe.
And they all go marching down to the town
in the rain, in the rain.

Rat a tat-tat! Rat a tat-tat! Ba-rump, ba-rump, ba-rump!

The aunts go marching three by three, hurrah! Hurrah!
The aunts go marching three by three, hurrah! Hurrah!
The aunts go marching three by three.
The little one stops to look and see.
And they all go marching down to the town
in the rain, in the rain.

Rat a tat-tat! Rat a tat-tat! Ba-rump, ba-rump, ba-rump!

The aunts go marching four by four, hurrah! Hurrah!
The aunts go marching four by four, hurrah! Hurrah!
The aunts go marching four by four.
The little one stops to take one more.
And they all go marching down to the town
in the rain, in the rain.

Rat a tat-tat! Rat a tat-tat! Ba-rump, ba-rump, ba-rump!

The aunts go marching five by five, hurrah! Hurrah!
The aunts go marching five by five, hurrah! Hurrah!
The aunts go marching five by five.
The little one stops to shout, "SURPRISE!"
And they all go marching down to the town
in the rain, in the rain.

Rat a tat-tat!
Rat a tat-tat!
Ba-rump, ba-rump, ba-rump!

The aunts go marching six by six, hurrah! Hurrah!
The aunts go marching six by six, hurrah! Hurrah!
The aunts go marching six by six.
The little one stops to pick up her sticks.
And they all go marching down to the town
in the rain, in the rain.

Rat a tat-tat!
Rat a tat-tat!
Ba-rump, ba-rump, ba-rump!

The aunts go marching seven by seven, hurrah! Hurrah!
The aunts go marching seven by seven, hurrah! Hurrah!
The aunts go marching seven by seven.
The little one stops to look at the heavens.

Rat a tat-tat! Rat a tat-tat! Ba-rump, ba-rump, ba-rump!

The aunts come marching eight by eight, hurrah! Hurrah!
The aunts come marching eight by eight, hurrah! Hurrah!
The aunts come marching eight by eight.
The little one runs to open the gate.
And they all come marching back from the town
in the rain, in the rain.

Rat a tat-tat! Rat a tat-tat!
Ba-rump, ba-rump, ba-rump!
BOOM!

The aunts come marching nine by nine, hurrah! Hurrah!
The aunts come marching nine by nine, hurrah! Hurrah!
The aunts come marching nine by nine.
The little one runs to join the line.
And they all come marching back from the town
in the rain, in the rain.

Rat a tat-tat!
Rat a tat-tat!
Ba-rump, ba-rump, ba-rump!

BOOM!

The aunts come marching ten by ten, hurrah! Hurrah!
The aunts come marching ten by ten, hurrah! Hurrah!
The aunts come marching ten by ten. . . .

The little one says, "Let's do it again!"
In the rain, in the rain.

Rat a tat-tat!
Rat a tat-tat!
Ba-rump,
ba-rump,
ba-rump!

BOOM!